Let's Play Tag!

Read the Page

Say It Sound It Spell It

Game

Repeat

Stop

Why is wh yellow?

Yellow highlights represent letter teams that make a single sound or words with irregular decoding patterns.

INTERNET CONNECTION REQUIRED FOR AUDIO DOWNLOAD.
To use this book with the Tag™ Reader, you must first download audio from the LeapFrog® Connect Application.
The LeapFrog Connect Application can be installed from the CD provided with your Tag Reader or at leapfrog.com/tag.

The Fix-It Kid

Story by Suzanne Barchers
Illustrated by TRP Toons and Yakovetic Productions

Leap got a gift, a big tool kit.

Leap will fix it all,
bit by bit.

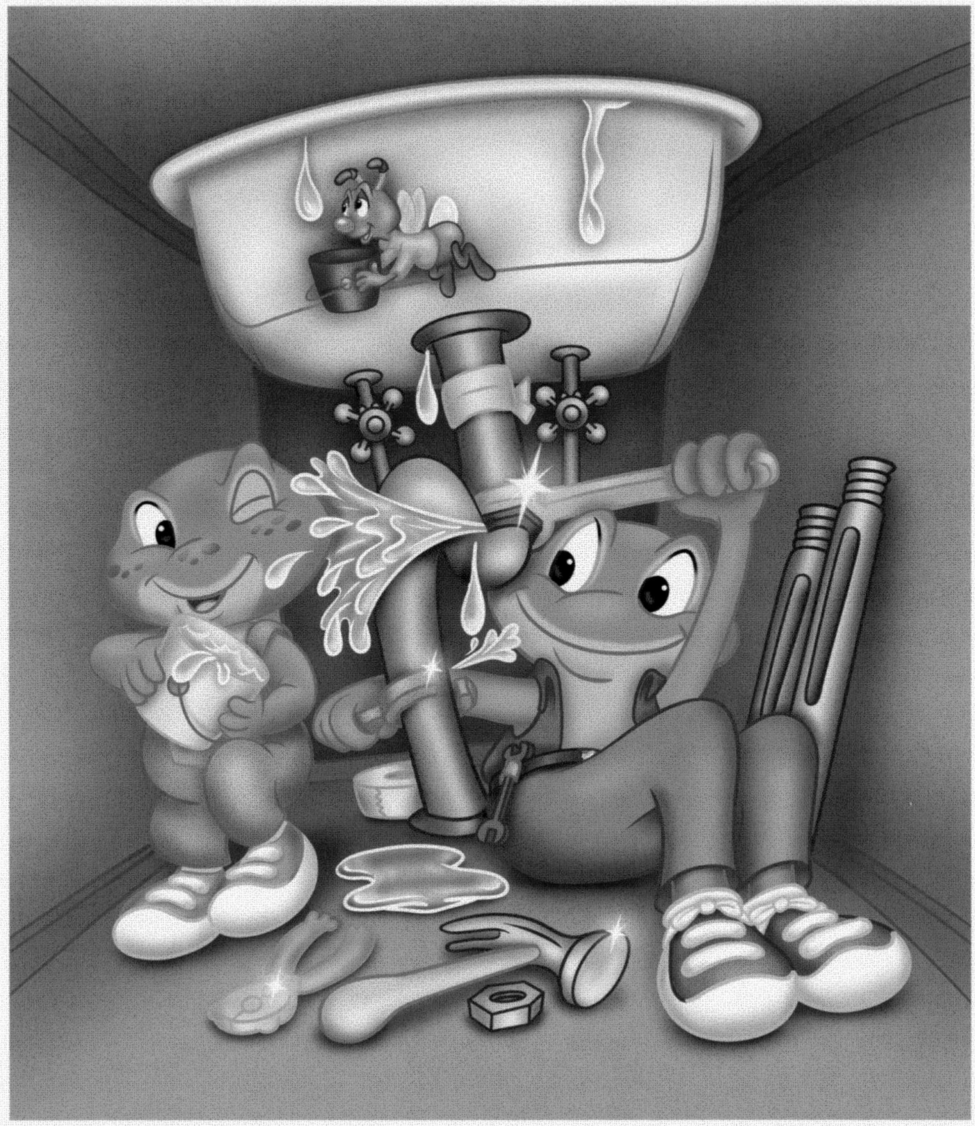

Leap will fix the sink. He will fix the drip.

With his big, big,
pin, he will fix
the rip.

Leap will fix the clock. He will make it tick.

Leap will fix the lock. He will make it click.

Leap will fix the lamp. It will soon be lit.

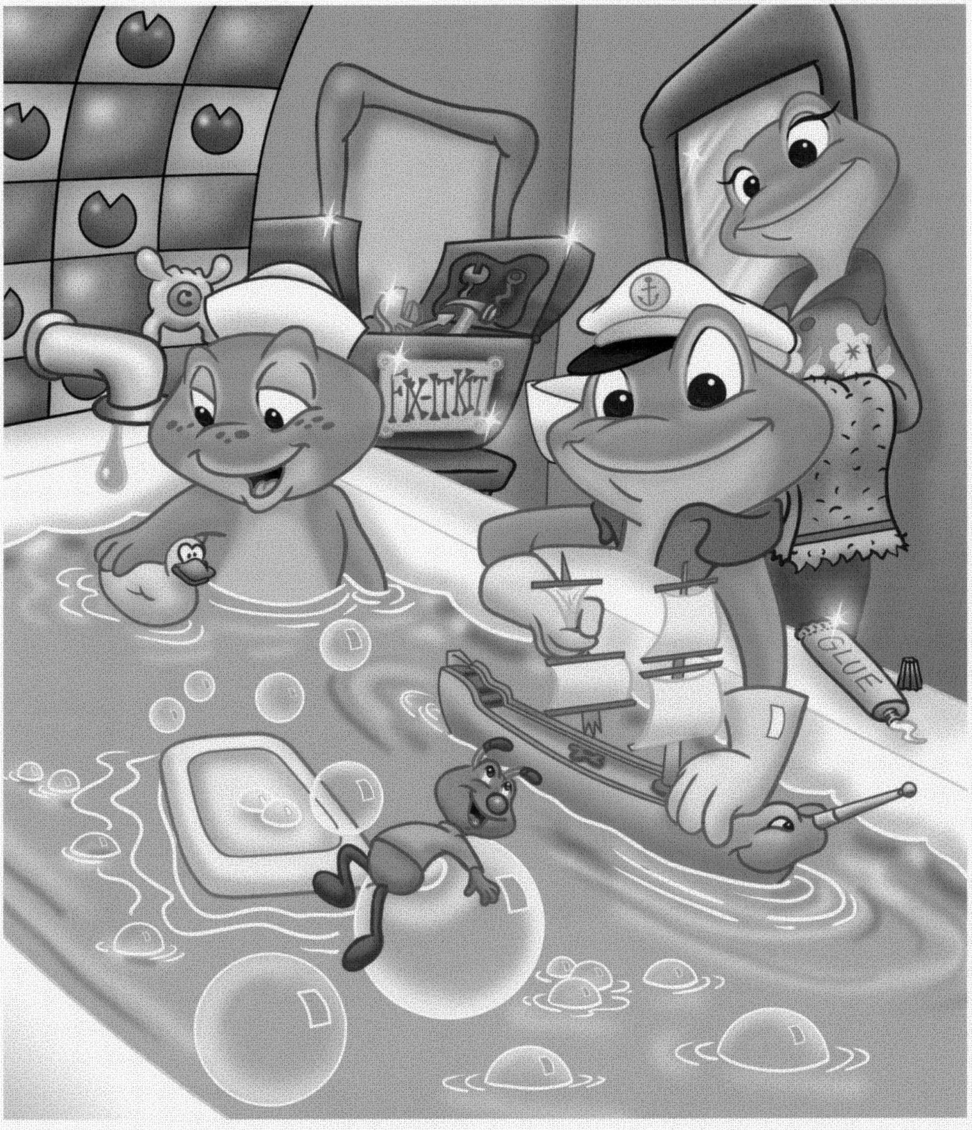

Leap will fix the
ship, with his
fix-it kit.

Can Leap fix a pig?
Can he fix a fish?

Can Leap fix a swing? Can he fix a dish?

Leap can fix it all.
Look at what he did.
He fixed it in a zip.
Leap's a fix-it kid!

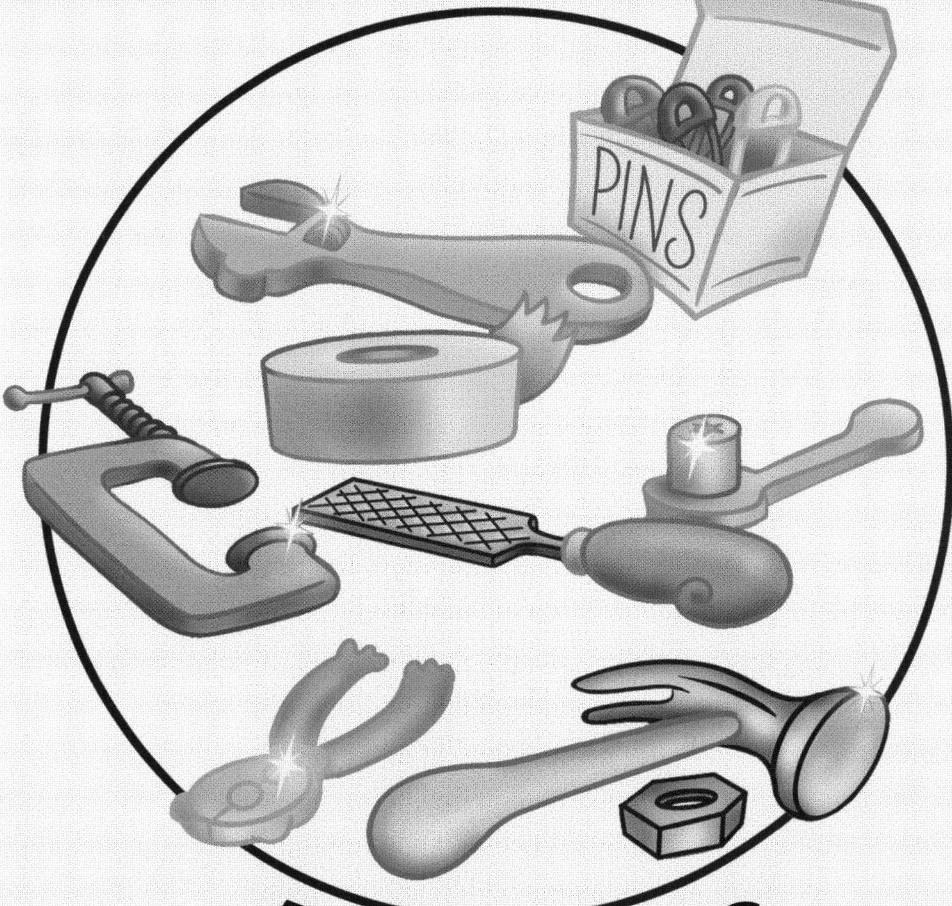

Activities

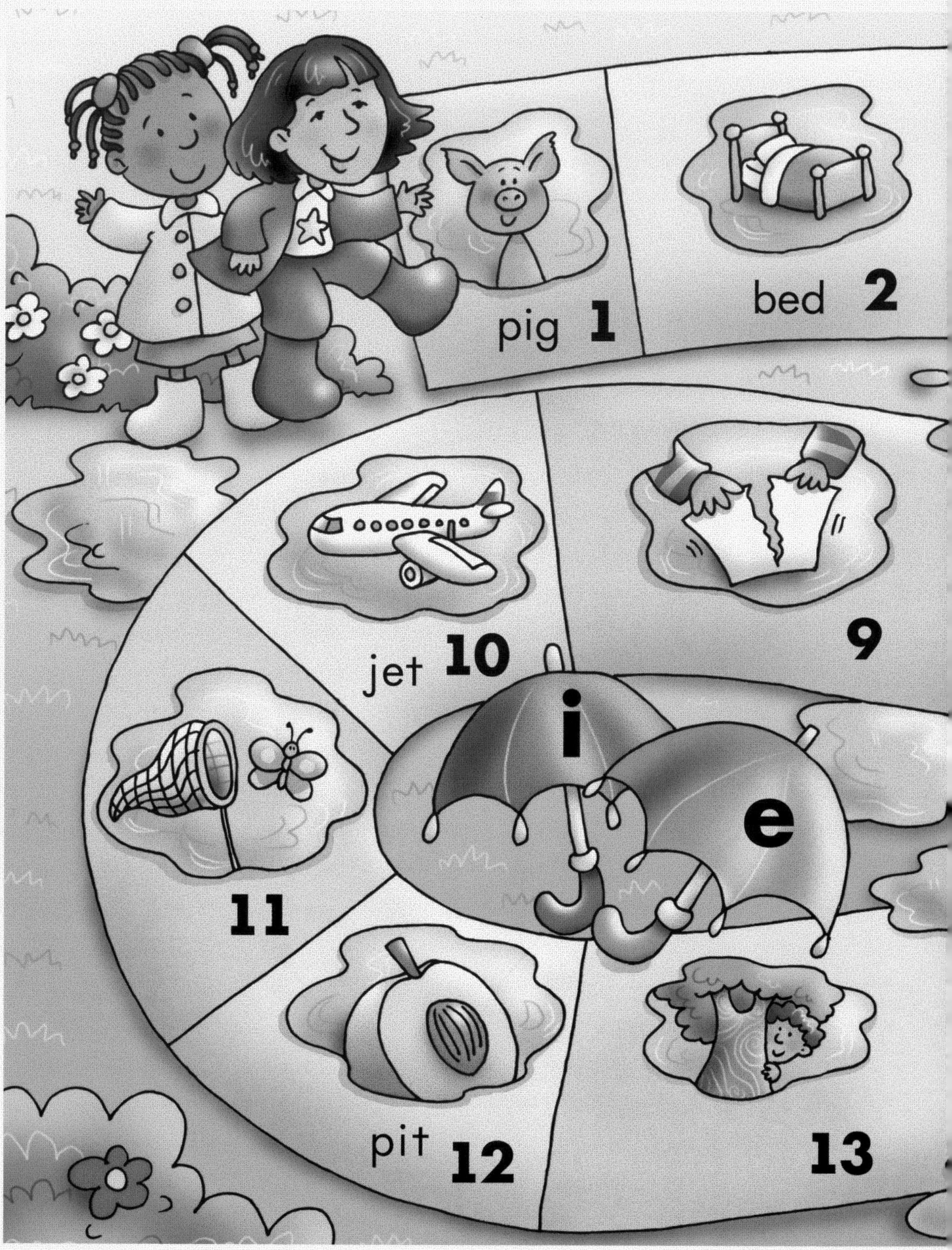
pig 1
bed 2
9
jet 10
11
pit 12
13
i
e

3
wig 4
5
fed 6
7
hen 8
rim 14
15
dig 16

ten
tin
pin
led
pen
lid
set
bet
sit
bit

z
i
d
b
g
l
n
e
p
t

Words You're Learning

Short Vowels

Short i Words

big	his	kit	rip
bit	in	lit	will
did	it	pig	zip
fix	kid	pin	

Sight Words

all	what
the	with

Challenging Words

click	fixed	sink	tick
drip	gift	soon	tool
fish	ship	swing	